Boy on the Brink

Boy on the Brink

David McPhail

Henry Holt and Company

New York

For Jan, whose encouragement and faith
made it all possible,
and for Laura and Patrick,
true believers

Henry Holt and Company, LLC
Publishers since 1866
175 Fifth Avenue
New York, New York 10010
www.henryholtchildrensbooks.com

Library of Congress Cataloging-in-Publication Data
McPhail, David.
Boy on the brink / David McPhail.—1st ed.
p.   cm.
Summary: After a day during which his various relatives urge him to be careful,
a young boy experiences a nightful of heroic adventures in his dreams.
ISBN-13: 978-0-8050-7618-9
ISBN-10: 0-8050-7618-2
[1. Dreams—Fiction. 2. Adventure and adventurers—Fiction.] I. Title.
PZ7.M4788184Boy 2006   [E]—dc22   2005016685

First Edition—2006 / Designed by Patrick Collins
The artist used watercolor and ink on illustration board to create the illustrations for this book.
Printed in China on acid-free paper. ∞

1 3 5 7 9 10 8 6 4 2

What a day!

Early in the morning the boy went fishing with his
grandfather.

"Not too close," his grandfather warned. "It's a
long way down."

On the ride back they waited at a railroad crossing
while a speeding train thundered by.

"Unstoppable," said his grandfather wistfully.

The boy arrived home just in time to join his family for a day at the beach.

"Stay out of the caves," his mother said when the boy went to explore.

"And keep an eye on your sister," added his father.

When the tide went out the boy took his toy boat down to the edge of the water.

"Watch out for sharks!" teased his cousin.

That evening the boy and his sister went to a
carnival in the park, where their aunt and uncle
treated them to a pony ride.

"Hold on tight," said their uncle.
"You don't want to fall off," said their aunt.

By the time they returned home the boy was exhausted.

"Pleasant dreams, dear," his mother said as she tucked him in and turned off the light.

That night there was a storm. Thunder shook the boy's bed and sent it flying . . .

. . . and when the bed landed, it was transformed into a world of mountains and valleys, with a river that spilled into a waterfall and into a vast green sea.

In the distance a pony was grazing, and when the boy whistled the pony came running.

The boy leaped onto the pony's back and galloped off into the high hills.

As they raced along a narrow ledge the pony loosened a pebble that dislodged a stone that bumped a boulder and sent it careening down the gorge—while far below a truck loaded with bananas was coming around the bend.

—⟋⟍⟋—

Higher up the trail was a castle where a yellow-haired girl was calling for help.

The boy swung across the canyon on his cowboy rope to rescue her before the castle guards could be alerted.

—⟋⟍⟋—

The sturdy pony carried them to the top of the tallest mountain.

Suddenly the ground began to shake and the mountain split in two—just as a train was approaching.

—✽—

Farther down the trail they crossed a dam with a crack in it that the boy patched with some gum. He wondered if it would hold.

—✽—

As they came around the bend they saw a ship teetering at the edge of a waterfall.

The boy lassoed the propeller to keep the ship from plunging into the sea.

—m—

—⟊—

After saying good-bye to the pony and the yellow-haired girl, the boy slid down to the beach, where he discovered a huge cave. He wanted to go in and search through the treasures, but a narrow band of dark water stood in his way.

—⟊—

The beach was rapidly disappearing under the incoming tide, so the boy climbed the cliffs and made his way along the path to the top.

Things started to look familiar to the boy, but as he glanced around he stumbled and fell—

"Breakfast, Jim!" his mother announced from the top of the stairs.

And then he was awake.

The boy dressed, then dashed downstairs to the smell of banana pancakes and slid into the warm empty seat at the end of the table.

What a night!